# PERCY

# A TRAGEDY

# IN FIVE ACTS

# BY MRS. HANNAH MORE

## REMARKS.

This tragedy, in which Mrs. Hannah More is supposed to have been assisted by Garrick, was produced at Covent Garden Theatre, in 1778, with success; and revived, in 1818, at the same Theatre.

The feuds of the rival houses of Percy and of Douglas have furnished materials for this melancholy tale, in which Mrs. More1 has embodied many judicious sentiments and excellent passages, producing a forcible lesson to parental tyranny. The victim of her husband's unreasonable jealousy, Elwina's virtuous conflict is pathetic and interesting; while Percy's sufferings, and the vain regret of Earl Raby, excite and increase our sympathy.

## DRAMATIS PERSONÆ.

| | |
|---|---|
| Percy, Earl of Northumberland | Mr. Lewis. |
| Earl Douglas | Mr. Wroughton. |
| Earl Raby, Elwina's Father | Mr. Aickin. |
| Edric, Friend to Douglas | Mr. Whitefield. |
| Harcourt, Friend to Percy | Mr. Robson. |
| Sir Hubert, a Knight | Mr. Hull. |

| | |
|---|---|
| Elwina | Mrs. Barry. |
| Birtha | Mrs. Jackson. |

Knights, Guards, Attendants, &c.
scene,—Raby Castle, in Durham.

## PERCY.

## ACT THE FIRST.

### SCENE I. A GOTHIC HALL.

Enter Edric and Birtha.

*Bir.* What may this mean? Earl Douglas has enjoin'd thee
To meet him here in private?

*Edr.* Yes, my sister,
And this injunction I have oft receiv'd;
But when he comes, big with some painful secret,
He starts, looks wild, then drops ambiguous hints,
Frowns, hesitates, turns pale, and says 'twas nothing;
Then feigns to smile, and by his anxious care
To prove himself at ease, betrays his pain.

Bir. Since my short sojourn here, I've mark'd this earl,
And though the ties of blood unite us closely,
I shudder at his haughtiness of temper,
Which not his gentle wife, the bright Elwina,
Can charm to rest. Ill are their spirits pair'd;
His is the seat of frenzy, her's of softness,
His love is transport, her's is trembling duty;
Rage in his soul is as the whirlwind fierce,
While her's ne'er felt the power of that rude passion.

Edr. Perhaps the mighty soul of Douglas mourns,
Because inglorious love detains him here,
While our bold knights, beneath the Christian standard,
Press to the bulwarks of Jerusalem.

Bir. Though every various charm adorns Elwina,
And though the noble Douglas dotes to madness,
Yet some dark mystery involves their fate:
The canker grief devours Elwina's bloom,
And on her brow meek resignation sits,
Hopeless, yet uncomplaining.

Edr. 'Tis most strange.

Bir. Once, not long since, she thought herself alone;
'Twas then the pent-up anguish burst its bounds;
With broken voice, clasp'd hands, and streaming eyes,
She call'd upon her father, call'd him cruel,
And said her duty claim'd far other recompence.

Edr. Perhaps the absence of the good Lord Raby,
Who, at her nuptials, quitted this fair castle,
Resigning it to her, may thus afflict her.
Hast thou e'er question'd her, good Birtha?

Bir. Often,
But hitherto in vain; and yet she shews me
The endearing kindness of a sister's love;
But if I speak of Douglas——

Edr. See! he comes.
It would offend him should he find you here.

Enter Douglas.

Dou. How! Edric and his sister in close conference?
Do they not seem alarm'd at my approach?
And see, how suddenly they part! Now Edric,[exit Birtha.

2

Was this well done? or was it like a friend,
When I desir'd to meet thee here alone;
With all the warmth of trusting confidence,
To lay my bosom naked to thy view,
And shew thee all its weakness, was it well
To call thy sister here, to let her witness
Thy friend's infirmity?—perhaps to tell her—

Edr. My lord, I nothing know; I came to learn.

Dou. Nay then thou dost suspect there's something wrong?

Edr. If we were bred from infancy together,
If I partook in all thy youthful griefs,
And every joy thou knew'st was doubly mine,
Then tell me all the secret of thy soul:
Or have these few short months of separation,
The only absence we have ever known,
Have these so rent the bands of love asunder,
That Douglas should distrust his Edric's truth?

Dou. My friend, I know thee faithful as thou'rt brave,
And I will trust thee—but not now, good Edric,
'Tis past, 'tis gone, it is not worth the telling,
'Twas wrong to cherish what disturb'd my peace;
I'll think of it no more.

Edr. Transporting news!
I fear'd some hidden trouble vex'd your quiet.
In secret I have watch'd——

Dou. Ha! watch'd in secret?
A spy, employ'd, perhaps, to note my actions.
What have I said? Forgive me, thou art noble:
Yet do not press me to disclose my grief,
For when thou know'st it, I perhaps shall hate thee
As much, my Edric, as I hate myself
For my suspicions—I am ill at ease.

Edr. How will the fair Elwina grieve to hear it!

Dou. Hold, Edric, hold—thou hast touch'd the fatal string
That wakes me into madness. Hear me then,
But let the deadly secret be secur'd
With bars of adamant in thy close breast.
Think on the curse which waits on broken oaths;
A knight is bound by more than vulgar ties,
And perjury in thee were doubly damn'd.
Well then, the king of England—

3

Edr. Is expected
From distant Palestine.

Dou. Forbid it, Heaven!
For with him comes—

Edr. Ah! who?

Dou. Peace, peace,
For see Elwina's here. Retire, my Edric;
When next we meet, thou shalt know all. Farewell.[exit Edric.
Now to conceal with care my bosom's anguish,
And let her beauty chase away my sorrows!
Yes, I would meet her with a face of smiles—
But 'twill not be.

Enter Elwina.

Elw. Alas, 'tis ever thus!
Thus ever clouded is his angry brow.[aside.

Dou. I were too blest, Elwina, could I hope
You met me here by choice, or that your bosom
Shar'd the warm transports mine must ever feel
At your approach.

Elw. My lord, if I intrude,
The cause which brings me claims at least forgiveness:
I fear you are not well, and come, unbidden,
Except by faithful duty, to inquire,
If haply in my power, my little power,
I have the means to minister relief
To your affliction?

Dou. What unwonted goodness!
O I were blest above the lot of man,
If tenderness, not duty, brought Elwina;
Cold, ceremonious, and unfeeling duty,
That wretched substitute for love: but know,
The heart demands a heart; nor will be paid
With less than what it gives. E'en now, Elwina,
The glistening tear stands trembling in your eyes,
Which cast their mournful sweetness on the ground,
As if they fear'd to raise their beams to mine,
And read the language of reproachful love.

Elw. My lord, I hop'd the thousand daily proofs
Of my obedience——

4

Dou. Death to all my hopes!
Heart-rending word!—obedience? what's obedience?
'Tis fear, 'tis hate, 'tis terror, 'tis aversion,
'Tis the cold debt of ostentatious duty,
Paid with insulting caution, to remind me
How much you tremble to offend a tyrant
So terrible as Douglas.—O, Elwina——
While duty measures the regard it owes
With scrupulous precision and nice justice,
Love never reasons, but profusely gives,
Gives, like a thoughtless prodigal, its all,
And trembles then, lest it has done too little.

Elw. Indeed I'm most unhappy that my cares,
And my solicitude to please, offend.

Dou. True tenderness is less solicitous,
Less prudent and more fond; the enamour'd heart,
Conscious it loves, and blest in being lov'd,
Reposes on the object it adores,
And trusts the passion it inspires and feels.—
Thou hast not learnt how terrible it is
To feed a hopeless flame.—But hear, Elwina,
Thou most obdurate, hear me.—

Elw. Say, my lord,
For your own lips shall vindicate my fame,
Since at the altar I became your wife,
Can malice charge me with an act, a word,
I ought to blush at? Have I not still liv'd
As open to the eye of observation,
As fearless innocence should ever live?
I call attesting angels to be witness,
If in my open deed, or secret thought,
My conduct, or my heart, they've aught discern'd
Which did not emulate their purity.

Dou. This vindication ere you were accus'd,
This warm defence, repelling all attacks
Ere they are made, and construing casual words
To formal accusations, trust me, madam,
Shews rather an alarm'd and vigilant spirit,
For ever on the watch to guard its secret,
Than the sweet calm of fearless innocence.
Who talk'd of guilt? Who testified suspicion?

Elw. Learn, sir, that virtue, while 'tis free from blame,
Is modest, lowly, meek, and unassuming;

Not apt, like fearful vice, to shield its weakness
Beneath the studied pomp of boastful phrase
Which swells to hide the poverty it shelters;
But, when this virtue feels itself suspected,
Insulted, set at nought, its whiteness stain'd,
It then grows proud, forgets its humble worth,
And rates itself above its real value.

Dou. I did not mean to chide! but think, O think,
What pangs must rend this fearful doting heart,
To see you sink impatient of the grave,
To feel, distracting thought! to feel you hate me!

Elw. What if the slender thread by which I hold
This poor precarious being soon must break,
Is it Elwina's crime, or heaven's decree?
Yet I shall meet, I trust, the king of terrors,
Submissive and resign'd, without one pang,
One fond regret, at leaving this gay world.

Dou. Yes, madam, there is one, one man ador'd,
For whom your sighs will heave, your tears will flow,
For whom this hated world will still be dear,
For whom you still would live——

Elw. Hold, hold, my lord,
What may this mean?

Dou. Ah! I have gone too far.
What have I said?—Your father, sure, your father,
The good Lord Raby, may at least expect
One tender sigh.

Elw. Alas, my lord! I thought
The precious incense of a daughter's sighs
Might rise to heaven, and not offend its ruler.

Dou. 'Tis true; yet Raby is no more belov'd
Since he bestow'd his daughter's hand on Douglas:
That was a crime the dutiful Elwina
Can never pardon; and believe me, madam,
My love's so nice, so delicate my honour,
I am asham'd to owe my happiness
To ties which make you wretched.[exit Douglas.

Elw. Ah! how's this?
Though I have ever found him fierce and rash,
Full of obscure surmises and dark hints,
Till now he never ventur'd to accuse me.

6

Yet there is one, one man belov'd, ador'd,
For whom your tears will flow—these were his words—
And then the wretched subterfuge of, Raby—
How poor th' evasion!—But my Birtha comes.

Enter Birtha.

Bir. Crossing the portico I met Lord Douglas,
Disorder'd were his looks, his eyes shot fire;
He call'd upon your name with such distraction,
I fear'd some sudden evil had befallen you.

Elw. Not sudden: no; long has the storm been gathering,
Which threatens speedily to burst in ruin
On this devoted head.

Bir. I ne'er beheld
Your gentle soul so ruffled, yet I've mark'd you,
While others thought you happiest of the happy,
Blest with whate'er the world calls great, or good,
With all that nature, all that fortune gives,
I've mark'd you bending with a weight of sorrow.

Elw. O I will tell thee all! thou couldst not find
An hour, a moment in Elwina's life,
When her full heart so long'd to ease its burthen,
And pour its sorrows in thy friendly bosom:
Hear then, with pity hear, my tale of woe,
And, O forgive, kind nature, filial piety,
If my presumptuous lips arraign a father!
Yes, Birtha, that belov'd, that cruel father,
Has doom'd me to a life of hopeless anguish,
To die of grief ere half my days are number'd;
Doom'd me to give my trembling hand to Douglas,
'Twas all I had to give—my heart was—Percy's.

Bir. What do I hear?

Elw. My misery, not my crime.
Long since the battle 'twixt the rival houses
Of Douglas and of Percy, for whose hate
This mighty globe's too small a theatre,
One summer's morn my father chas'd the deer
On Cheviot Hills, Northumbria's fair domain.

Bir. On that fam'd spot where first the feuds commenc'd
Between the earls?

Elw. The same. During the chace,

7

Some of my father's knights receiv'd an insult
From the Lord Percy's herdsmen, churlish foresters,
Unworthy of the gentle blood they serv'd.
My father, proud and jealous of his honour,
(Thou know'st the fiery temper of our barons,)
Swore that Northumberland had been concern'd
In this rude outrage, nor would hear of peace,
Or reconcilement, which the Percy offer'd;
But bade me hate, renounce, and banish him.
O! 'twas a task too hard for all my duty:
I strove, and wept; I strove—but still I lov'd.

Bir. Indeed 'twas most unjust; but say what follow'd?

Elw. Why should I dwell on the disastrous tale?
Forbid to see me, Percy soon embark'd
With our great king against the Saracen.
Soon as the jarring kingdoms were at peace,
Earl Douglas, whom till then I ne'er had seen,
Came to this castle; 'twas my hapless fate
To please him.—Birtha! thou can'st tell what follow'd:
But who shall tell the agonies I felt?
My barbarous father forc'd me to dissolve
The tender vows himself had bid me form——
He dragg'd me trembling, dying, to the altar,
I sigh'd, I struggled, fainted, and complied.

Bir. Did Douglas know, a marriage had been once
Propos'd 'twixt you and Percy?

Elw. If he did,
He thought, like you, it was a match of policy,
Nor knew our love surpass'd our fathers' prudence.

Bir. Should he now find he was the instrument
Of the Lord Raby's vengeance?

Elw. 'Twere most dreadful!
My father lock'd this motive in his breast,
And feign'd to have forgot the chace of Cheviot.
Some moons have now completed their slow course
Since my sad marriage.—Percy still is absent.

Bir. Nor will return before his sov'reign comes.

Elw. Talk not of his return! this coward heart
Can know no thought of peace but in his absence.
How, Douglas here again? some fresh alarm!

Enter Douglas, agitated, with letters in his hand.

Dou. Madam, your pardon—

Elw. What disturbs my lord?

Dou. Nothing.—Disturb! I ne'er was more at ease.
These letters from your father give us notice
He will be here to-night:—He further adds,
The king's each hour expected.

Elw. How? the king?
Said you, the king?

Dou. And 'tis Lord Raby's pleasure
That you among the foremost bid him welcome.
You must attend the court.

Elw. Must I, my lord?

Dou. Now to observe how she receives the news![aside.

Elw. I must not,—cannot.—By the tender love
You have so oft profess'd for poor Elwina,
Indulge this one request—O let me stay!

Dou. Enchanting sounds! she does not wish to go—[aside.

Elw. The bustling world, the pomp which waits on greatness,
Ill suits my humble, unambitious soul;—
Then leave me here, to tread the safer path
Of private life; here, where my peaceful course
Shall be as silent as the shades around me;
Nor shall one vagrant wish be e'er allow'd
To stray beyond the bounds of Raby Castle.

Dou. O music to my ears! [aside.] Can you resolve
To hide those wond'rous beauties in the shade,
Which rival kings would cheaply buy with empire?
Can you renounce the pleasures of a court,
Whose roofs resound with minstrelsy and mirth?

Elw. My lord, retirement is a wife's best duty,
And virtue's safest station is retreat.

Dou. My soul's in transports! [aside] But can you forego
What wins the soul of woman—admiration?
A world, where charms inferior far to yours
Only presume to shine when you are absent!

9

Will you not long to meet the public gaze?
Long to eclipse the fair, and charm the brave?

Elw. These are delights in which the mind partakes not.

Dou. I'll try her farther.[aside.
[takes her hand, and looks stedfastly at her as he speaks.
But reflect once more:
When you shall hear that England's gallant peers,
Fresh from the fields of war, and gay with glory,
All vain with conquest, and elate with fame,
When you shall hear these princely youths contend,
In many a tournament, for beauty's prize;
When you shall hear of revelry and masking,
Of mimic combats and of festive halls,
Of lances shiver'd in the cause of love,
Will you not then repent, then wish your fate,
Your happier fate, had till that hour reserv'd you
For some plumed conqueror?

Elw. My fate, my lord,
Is now bound up with yours.

Dou. Here let me kneel—
Yes, I will kneel, and gaze, and weep, and wonder;
Thou paragon of goodness!—pardon, pardon,[kisses her hand.
I am convinc'd—I can no longer doubt,
Nor talk, nor hear, nor reason, nor reflect.
—I must retire, and give a loose to joy.[exit Douglas.

Bir. The king returns.

Elw. And with him Percy comes!

Bir. You needs must go.

Elw. Shall I solicit ruin,
And pull destruction on me ere its time?
I, who have held it criminal to name him?
I will not go—I disobey thee, Douglas,
But disobey thee to preserve thy honour.[exeunt.

ACT THE SECOND.

SCENE I. THE HALL.

Enter Douglas, speaking.

See that the traitor instantly be seiz'd,
And strictly watch'd: let none have access to him.—
O jealousy, thou aggregate of woes!
Were there no hell, thy torments would create one.
But yet she may be guiltless—may? she must.
How beautiful she look'd! pernicious beauty!
Yet innocent as bright seem'd the sweet blush
That mantled on her cheek. But not for me,
But not for me, those breathing roses blow!
And then she wept—What! can I bear her tears?
Well—let her weep—her tears are for another;
O did they fall for me, to dry their streams
I'd drain the choicest blood that feeds this heart,
Nor think the drops I shed were half so precious.
[he stands in a musing posture.

Enter Lord Raby.

Raby. Sure I mistake—am I in Raby Castle?
Impossible; that was the seat of smiles;
And Cheerfulness and Joy were household gods.
I us'd to scatter pleasures when I came,
And every servant shar'd his lord's delight;
But now Suspicion and Distrust dwell here,
And Discontent maintains a sullen sway.
Where is the smile unfeign'd, the jovial welcome,
Which cheer'd the sad, beguil'd the pilgrim's pain,
And made Dependency forget its bonds?
Where is the antient, hospitable hall,
Whose vaulted roof once rung with harmless mirth,
Where every passing stranger was a guest,
And every guest a friend? I fear me much,
If once our nobles scorn their rural seats,
Their rural greatness, and their vassals' love,
Freedom and English grandeur are no more.

Dou. [advancing.] My lord, you are welcome.

Raby. Sir, I trust I am;
But yet methinks I shall not feel I'm welcome
Till my Elwina bless me with her smiles:
She was not wont with ling'ring step to meet me,
Or greet my coming with a cold embrace;
Now, I extend my longing arms in vain;
My child, my darling, does not come to fill them.
O they were happy days, when she would fly
To meet me from the camp, or from the chace,

11

And with her fondness overpay my toils!
How eager would her tender hands unbrace
The ponderous armour from my war-worn limbs,
And pluck the helmet which oppos'd her kiss!

Dou. O sweet delights, that never must be mine!

Raby. What do I hear?

Dou. Nothing: inquire no farther.

Raby. My lord, if you respect an old man's peace,
If e'er you doted on my much-lov'd child,
As 'tis most sure you made me think you did,
Then, by the pangs which you may one day feel,
When you, like me, shall be a fond, fond father,
And tremble for the treasure of your age,
Tell me what this alarming silence means?
You sigh, you do not speak, nay more, you hear not;
Your lab'ring soul turns inward on itself,
As there were nothing but your own sad thoughts
Deserv'd regard. Does my child live?

Dou. She does.

Raby. To bless her father!

Dou. And to curse her husband!

Raby. Ah! have a care, my lord, I'm not so old—

Dou. Nor I so base, that I should tamely bear it;
Nor am I so inur'd to infamy,
That I can say, without a burning blush,
She lives to be my curse!

Raby. How's this?

Dou. I thought
The lily opening to the heaven's soft dews,
Was not so fragrant, and was not so chaste.

Raby. Has she prov'd otherwise? I'll not believe it,
Who has traduc'd my sweet, my innocent child?
Yet she's too good to 'scape calumnious tongues.
I know that Slander loves a lofty mark:
It saw her soar a flight above her fellows,
And hurl'd its arrow to her glorious height,
To reach her heart, and bring her to the ground.

12

Dou. Had the rash tongue of Slander so presum'd,
My vengeance had not been of that slow sort
To need a prompter; nor should any arm,
No, not a father's, dare dispute with mine,
The privilege to die in her defence.
None dares accuse Elwina, but—

Raby. But who?

Dou. But Douglas.

Raby. [puts his hand to his sword.]
You?—O spare my age's weakness!
You do not know what 'tis to be a father;
You do not know, or you would pity me,
The thousand tender throbs, the nameless feelings,
The dread to ask, and yet the wish to know,
When we adore and fear; but wherefore fear?
Does not the blood of Raby fill her veins?

Dou. Percy;—know'st thou that name?

Raby. How? What of Percy?

Dou. He loves Elwina, and, my curses on him!
He is belov'd again.

Raby. I'm on the rack!

Dou. Not the two Theban brothers bore each other
Such deep, such deadly hate as I and Percy.

Raby. But tell me of my child.

Dou. [not minding him.] As I and Percy!
When at the marriage rites, O rites accurs'd!
I seiz'd her trembling hand, she started back,
Cold horror thrill'd her veins, her tears flow'd fast.
Fool that I was, I thought 'twas maiden fear;
Dull, doting ignorance! beneath those terrors,
Hatred for me and love for Percy lurk'd.

Raby. What proof of guilt is this?

Dou. E'er since our marriage,
Our days have still been cold and joyless all;
Painful restraint, and hatred ill disguis'd,
Her sole return for all my waste of fondness.

13

This very morn I told her 'twas your will
She should repair to court; with all those graces,
Which first subdued my soul, and still enslave it,
She begg'd to stay behind in Raby Castle,
For courts and cities had no charms for her.
Curse my blind love! I was again ensnar'd,
And doted on the sweetness which deceiv'd me.
Just at the hour she thought I should be absent,
(For chance could ne'er have tim'd their guilt so well,)
Arriv'd young Harcourt, one of Percy's knights,
Strictly enjoin'd to speak to none but her;
I seiz'd the miscreant: hitherto he's silent,
But tortures soon shall force him to confess!

Raby. Percy is absent—They have never met.

Dou. At what a feeble hold you grasp for succour!
Will it content me that her person's pure?
No, if her alien heart dotes on another,
She is unchaste, were not that other Percy.
Let vulgar spirits basely wait for proof,
She loves another—'tis enough for Douglas.

Raby. Be patient.

Dou. Be a tame convenient husband,
And meanly wait for circumstantial guilt?
No—I am nice as the first Cæsar was,
And start at bare suspicion.[going.

Raby. [holding him.] Douglas, hear me;
Thou hast nam'd a Roman husband; if she's false,
I mean to prove myself a Roman father.[exit Douglas.
This marriage was my work, and thus I'm punish'd!

Enter Elwina.

Elw. Where is my father? let me fly to meet him,
O let me clasp his venerable knees,
And die of joy in his belov'd embrace!

Raby. [avoiding her embrace.] Elwina!

Elw. And is that all? so cold?

Raby. [sternly.] Elwina!

Elw. Then I'm undone indeed! How stern his looks!
I will not be repuls'd, I am your child,

14

The child of that dear mother you ador'd;
You shall not throw me off, I will grow here,
And, like the patriarch, wrestle for a blessing.

Raby. [holding her from him.]
Before I take thee in these aged arms,
Press thee with transport to this beating heart,
And give a loose to all a parent's fondness,
Answer, and see thou answer me as truly
As if the dread inquiry came from heaven,—
Does no interior sense of guilt confound thee?
Canst thou lay all thy naked soul before me?
Can thy unconscious eye encounter mine?
Canst thou endure the probe, and never shrink?
Can thy firm hand meet mine, and never tremble?
Art thou prepar'd to meet the rigid Judge?
Or to embrace the fond, the melting, father?

Elw. Mysterious Heaven! to what am I reserv'd!

Raby. Should some rash man, regardless of thy fame,
And in defiance of thy marriage vows,
Presume to plead a guilty passion for thee,
What would'st thou do?

Elw. What honour bids me do.

Raby. Come to my arms![they embrace.

Elw. My father!

Raby. Yes, Elwina,
Thou art my child—thy mother's perfect image.

Elw. Forgive these tears of mingled joy and doubt;
For why that question? who should seek to please
The desolate Elwina?

Raby. But if any
Should so presume, canst thou resolve to hate him,
Whate'er his name, whate'er his pride of blood,
Whate'er his former arrogant pretensions?

Elw. Ha!

Raby. Dost thou falter? Have a care, Elwina.

Elw. Sir, do not fear me: am I not your daughter?

15

Raby. Thou hast a higher claim upon thy honour;
Thou art Earl Douglas' wife.

Elw. [weeps.] I am, indeed!

Raby. Unhappy Douglas!

Elw. Has he then complain'd?
Has he presum'd to sully my white fame?

Raby. He knows that Percy——

Elw. Was my destin'd husband;
By your own promise, by a father's promise,
And by a tie more strong, more sacred still,
Mine, by the fast firm bond of mutual love.

Raby. Now, by my fears, thy husband told me truth.

Elw. If he has told thee, that thy only child
Was forc'd a helpless victim to the altar,
Torn from his arms who had her virgin heart,
And forc'd to make false vows to one she hated,
Then I confess that he has told the truth.

Raby. Her words are barbed arrows in my heart.
But 'tis too late. [aside.] Thou hast appointed Harcourt
To see thee here by stealth in Douglas' absence?

Elw. No, by my life, nor knew I till this moment
That Harcourt was return'd. Was it for this
I taught my heart to struggle with its feelings?
Was it for this I bore my wrongs in silence?
When the fond ties of early love were broken,
Did my weak soul break out in fond complaints?
Did I reproach thee? Did I call thee cruel?
No—I endur'd it all; and wearied Heaven
To bless the father who destroy'd my peace.

Enter Messenger.

Mes. My lord, a knight, Sir Hubert as I think,
But newly landed from the holy wars,
Entreats admittance.

Raby. Let the warrior enter.[exit Messenger.
All private interests sink at his approach;
All selfish cares be for a moment banish'd;
I've now no child, no kindred but my country.

16

Elw. Weak heart, be still, for what hast thou to fear?

Enter Sir Hubert.

Raby. Welcome, thou gallant knight! Sir Hubert, welcome!
Welcome to Raby Castle!—In one word,
Is the king safe? Is Palestine subdu'd?

Sir H. The king is safe, and Palestine subdu'd.

Raby. Blest be the God of armies! Now, Sir Hubert,
By all the saints, thou'rt a right noble knight!
O why was I too old for this crusade!
I think it would have made me young again,
Could I, like thee, have seen the hated crescent
Yield to the Christian cross.—How now, Elwina!
What! cold at news which might awake the dead?
If there's a drop in thy degenerate veins
That glows not now, thou art not Raby's daughter.
It is religion's cause, the cause of Heaven!

Elw. When policy assumes religion's name,
And wears the sanctimonious garb of faith
Only to colour fraud, and license murder,
War then is tenfold guilt.

Raby. Blaspheming girl!

Elw. 'Tis not the crosier, nor the pontiff's robe,
The saintly look, nor elevated eye,
Nor Palestine destroy'd, nor Jordan's banks
Deluged with blood of slaughter'd infidels;
No, nor the extinction of the eastern world,
Nor all the mad, pernicious, bigot rage
Of your crusades, can bribe that Power who sees
The motive with the act. O blind, to think
That cruel war can please the Prince of Peace!
He, who erects his altar in the heart,
Abhors the sacrifice of human blood,
And all the false devotion of that zeal
Which massacres the world he died to save.

Raby. O impious rage! If thou would'st shun my curse,
No more, I charge thee.—Tell me, good Sir Hubert,
Say, have our arms achiev'd this glorious deed,
(I fear to ask,) without much Christian bloodshed?

Elw. Now, Heaven support me![aside.

17

Sir H. My good lord of Raby,
Imperfect is the sum of human glory!
Would I could tell thee that the field was won,
Without the death of such illustrious knights
As make the high-flush'd cheek of victory pale.

Elw. Why should I tremble thus?[aside.

Raby. Who have we lost?

Sir H. The noble Clifford, Walsingham, and Grey,
Sir Harry Hastings, and the valiant Pembroke,
All men of choicest note.

Raby. O that my name
Had been enroll'd in such a list of heroes!
If I was too infirm to serve my country,
I might have prov'd my love by dying for her.

Elw. Were there no more?

Sir H. But few of noble blood.
But the brave youth who gain'd the palm of glory,
The flower of knighthood, and the plume of war,
Who bore his banner foremost in the field,
Yet conquer'd more by mercy than the sword,
Was Percy.

Elw. Then he lives![aside.

Raby. Did he? Did Percy?
O gallant boy, then I'm thy foe no more;
Who conquers for my country is my friend!
His fame shall add new glories to a house,
Where never maid was false, nor knight disloyal.

Sir H. You do embalm him, lady, with your tears:
They grace the grave of glory where he lies—
He died the death of honour.

Elw. Said'st thou—died?

Sir H. Beneath the towers of Solyma he fell.

Elw. Oh!

Sir H. Look to the lady.
[Elwina faints in her father's arms.

18

Raby. Gentle knight, retire——
'Tis an infirmity of nature in her,
She ever mourns at any tale of blood;
She will be well anon—mean time, Sir Hubert,
You'll grace our castle with your friendly sojourn.

Sir H. I must return with speed—health to the lady.[exit.

Raby. Look up, Elwina. Should her husband come!
Yet she revives not.

Enter Douglas.

Dou. Ha——Elwina fainting!
My lord, I fear you have too harshly chid her.
Her gentle nature could not brook your sternness.
She wakes, she stirs, she feels returning life.
My love![he takes her hand.

Elw. O Percy!

Dou. [starts.] Do my senses fail me?

Elw. My Percy, 'tis Elwina calls.

Dou. Hell, hell!

Raby. Retire awhile, my daughter.

Elw. Douglas here,
My father and my husband?—O for pity—
[exit, casting a look of anguish on both.

Dou. Now, now confess she well deserves my vengeance!
Before my face to call upon my foe!

Raby. Upon a foe who has no power to hurt thee—
Earl Percy's slain.

Dou. I live again.—But hold—
Did she not weep? she did, and wept for Percy.
If she laments him, he's my rival still,
And not the grave can bury my resentment.

Raby. The truly brave are still the truly gen'rous;
Now, Douglas, is the time to prove thee both.
If it be true that she did once love Percy,
Thou hast no more to fear, since he is dead.

19

Release young Harcourt, let him see Elwina,
'Twill serve a double purpose, 'twill at once
Prove Percy's death, and thy unchang'd affection.
Be gentle to my child, and win her heart
By confidence and unreproaching love.

Dou. By Heaven, thou counsel'st well! it shall be done.
Go set him free, and let him have admittance
To my Elwina's presence.

Raby. Farewell, Douglas.
Shew thou believ'st her faithful, and she'll prove so.[exit.

Dou. Northumberland is dead—that thought is peace!
Her heart may yet be mine, transporting hope!
Percy was gentle, even a foe avows it,
And I'll be milder than a summer's breeze.
Yes, thou most lovely, most ador'd of women,
I'll copy every virtue, every grace,
Of my bless'd rival, happier even in death
To be thus loved, than living to be scorn'd.[exit.

ACT THE THIRD.

SCENE I. A GARDEN AT RABY CASTLE, WITH A BOWER.

Enter Percy and Sir Hubert.

Sir H. That Percy lives, and is return'd in safety,
More joys my soul than all the mighty conquests
That sun beheld, which rose on Syria's ruin.

Per. I've told thee, good Sir Hubert, by what wonder
I was preserv'd, though number'd with the slain.

Sir H. 'Twas strange, indeed!

Per. 'Twas Heaven's immediate work!
But let me now indulge a dearer joy,
Talk of a richer gift of Mercy's hand;
A gift so precious to my doating heart,
That life preserv'd is but a second blessing.
O Hubert, let my soul indulge its softness!
The hour, the spot, is sacred to Elwina.
This was her fav'rite walk; I well remember,
(For who forgets that loves as I have lov'd?)

20

'Twas in that very bower she gave this scarf,
Wrought by the hand of love! she bound it on,
And, smiling, cried, Whate'er befal us, Percy,
Be this the sacred pledge of faith between us.
I knelt, and swore, call'd every power to witness,
No time, nor circumstance, should force it from me,
But I would lose my life and that together—
Here I repeat my vow.

Sir H. Is this the man
Beneath whose single arm an host was crush'd?
He, at whose name the Saracen turn'd pale?
And when he fell, victorious armies wept,
And mourn'd a conquest they had bought so dear?
How has he chang'd the trumpet's martial note,
And all the stirring clangor of the war,
For the soft melting of the lover's lute!
Why are thine eyes still bent upon the bower?

Per. O Hubert, Hubert, to a soul enamour'd,
There is a sort of local sympathy,
Which, when we view the scenes of early passion,
Paints the bright image of the object lov'd
In stronger colours than remoter scenes
Could ever paint it; realizes shade,
Dresses it up in all the charms it wore,
Talks to it nearer, frames its answers kinder,
Gives form to fancy, and embodies thought.

Sir H. I should not be believ'd in Percy's camp,
If I should tell them that their gallant leader,
The thunder of the war, the bold Northumberland,
Renouncing Mars, dissolv'd in amorous wishes,
Loiter'd in shades, and pin'd in rosy bowers,
To catch a transient gleam of two bright eyes.

Per. Enough of conquest, and enough of war!
Ambition's cloy'd—the heart resumes its rights.
When England's king, and England's good, requir'd,
This arm not idly the keen falchion brandish'd:
Enough—for vaunting misbecomes a soldier.
I live, I am return'd—am near Elwina!
Seest thou those turrets? Yes, that castle holds her;
But wherefore tell thee this? for thou hast seen her.
How look'd, what said she? Did she hear the tale
Of my imagin'd death without emotion?

Sir H. Percy, thou hast seen the musk-rose, newly blown,
Disclose its bashful beauties to the sun,

21

Till an unfriendly, chilling storm descended,
Crush'd all its blushing glories in their prime,
Bow'd its fair head, and blasted all its sweetness;
So droop'd the maid beneath the cruel weight
Of my sad tale.

Per. So tender and so true!

Sir H. I left her fainting in her father's arms,
The dying flower yet hanging on the tree.
Even Raby melted at the news I brought,
And envy'd thee thy glory.

Per. Then I am blest!
His hate subdued, I've nothing more to fear.

Sir H. My embassy dispatch'd, I left the castle,
Nor spoke to any of Lord Raby's household,
For fear the king should chide the tardiness
Of my return. My joy to find you living
You have already heard.

Per. But where is Harcourt?
Ere this he should have seen her, told her all,
How I surviv'd, return'd—and how I love!
I tremble at the near approach of bliss,
And scarcely can sustain the joy which waits me.

Sir H. Grant, Heaven, the fair one prove but half so true!

Per. O she is truth itself!

Sir H. She may be chang'd,
Spite of her tears, her fainting, and alarms.
I know the sex, know them as nature made 'em,
Not such as lovers wish and poets feign.

Per. To doubt her virtue were suspecting Heaven,
'Twere little less than infidelity!
And yet I tremble. Why does terror shake
These firm-strung nerves? But 'twill be ever thus,
When fate prepares us more than mortal bliss,
And gives us only human strength to bear it.

Sir H. What beam of brightness breaks through yonder gloom?

Per. Hubert—she comes! by all my hopes, she comes!
'Tis she—the blissful vision is Elwina!
But ah! what mean those tears?—She weeps for me!

22

O transport!—go.—I'll listen unobserv'd,
And for a moment taste the precious joy,
The banquet of a tear which falls for love.
[exit Sir Hubert. Percy goes into the bower.

Enter Elwina.

Shall I not weep? and have I then no cause?
If I could break the eternal bands of death,
And wrench the sceptre from his iron grasp;
If I could bid the yawning sepulchre
Restore to life its long committed dust;
If I could teach the slaughtering hand of war
To give me back my dear, my murder'd Percy,
Then I indeed might once more cease to weep.
[Percy comes out of the bower.

Per. Then cease, for Percy lives.

Elw. Protect me, Heaven!

Per. O joy unspeakable! My life, my love!
End of my toils, and crown of all my cares!
Kind as consenting peace, as conquest bright,
Dearer than arms, and lovelier than renown!

Elw. It is his voice—it is, it is, my Percy!
And dost thou live?

Per. I never liv'd till now.

Elw. And did my sighs, and did my sorrows, reach thee?
And art thou come at last to dry my tears?
How did'st thou 'scape the fury of the foe?

Per. Thy guardian genius hover'd o'er the field,
And turn'd the hostile spear from Percy's breast,
Lest thy fair image should be wounded there.
But Harcourt should have told thee all my fate,
How I surviv'd——

Elw. Alas! I have not seen him.
Oh! I have suffer'd much.

Per. Of that no more;
For every minute of our future lives
Shall be so bless'd, that we will learn to wonder
How we could ever think we were unhappy.

23

Elw. Percy—I cannot speak.

Per. Those tears how eloquent!
I would not change this motionless, mute, joy
For the sweet strains of angels: I look down
With pity on the rest of human kind,
However great may be their fame of happiness,
And think their niggard fate has given them nothing,
Not giving thee; or, granting some small blessing,
Denies them my capacity to feel it.

Elw. Alas! what mean you?

Per. Can I speak my meaning?
'Tis of such magnitude that words would wrong it;
But surely my Elwina's faithful bosom
Should beat in kind responses of delight,
And feel, but never question, what I mean.

Elw. Hold, hold, my heart, thou hast much more to suffer!

Per. Let the slow form, and tedious ceremony,
Wait on the splendid victims of ambition.
Love stays for none of these. Thy father's soften'd,
He will forget the fatal Cheviot chace;
Raby is brave, and I have serv'd my country;
I would not boast, it was for thee I conquer'd;
Then come, my love.

Elw. O never, never, never!

Per. Am I awake? Is that Elwina's voice?

Elw. Percy, thou most ador'd, and most deceiv'd!
If ever fortitude sustain'd thy soul,
When vulgar minds have sank beneath the stroke,
Let thy imperial spirit now support thee.—
If thou canst be so wond'rous merciful,
Do not, O do not, curse me!—but thou wilt,
Thou must—for I have done a fearful deed,
A deed of wild despair, a deed of horror.
I am, I am—

Per. Speak, say, what art thou?

Elw. Married!

Per. Oh!

Elw. Percy, I think I begg'd thee not to curse me;
But now I do revoke the fond petition.
Speak! ease thy bursting soul; reproach, upbraid,
O'erwhelm me with thy wrongs——I'll bear it all.

Per. Open, thou earth, and hide me from her sight!
Did'st thou not bid me curse thee?

Elw. Mercy! mercy!

Per. And have I 'scap'd the Saracen's fell sword
Only to perish by Elwina's guilt?
I would have bared my bosom to the foe,
I would have died, had I but known you wish'd it.

Elw. Percy, I lov'd thee most when most I wrong'd thee;
Yes, by these tears I did.

Per. Married! just Heaven!
Married! to whom? Yet wherefore should I know?
It cannot add fresh horrors to thy crime,
Or my destruction.

Elw. Oh! 'twill add to both.
How shall I tell? Prepare for something dreadful.
Hast thou not heard of—Douglas?

Per. Why 'tis well!
Thou awful Power, why waste thy wrath on me?
Why arm omnipotence to crush a worm?
I could have fallen without this waste of ruin.
Married to Douglas! By my wrongs, I like it;
'Tis perfidy complete, 'tis finish'd falsehood,
'Tis adding fresh perdition to the sin,
And filling up the measure of offence!

Elw. Oh! 'twas my father's deed! he made his child
An instrument of vengeance on thy head.
He wept and threaten'd, sooth'd me, and commanded.

Per. And you complied, most duteously complied!

Elw. I could withstand his fury; but his tears,
Ah, they undid me! Percy, dost thou know
The cruel tyranny of tenderness?
Hast thou e'er felt a father's warm embrace?
Hast thou e'er seen a father's flowing tears,
And known that thou could'st wipe those tears away?
If thou hast felt, and hast resisted these,

25

Then thou may'st curse my weakness; but if not,
Thou canst not pity, for thou canst not judge.

*Per.* Let me not hear the music of thy voice,
Or I shall love thee still; I shall forget
Thy fatal marriage and my savage wrongs.

*Elw.* Dost thou not hate me, Percy?

*Per.* Hate thee? Yes,
As dying martyrs hate the righteous cause
Of that bless'd power for whom they bleed—I hate thee.
[they look at each other with silent agony.]

Enter Harcourt.

*Har.* Forgive, my lord, your faithful knight——

*Per.* Come, Harcourt,
Come, and behold the wretch who once was Percy.

*Har.* With grief I've learn'd the whole unhappy tale.
Earl Douglas, whose suspicion never sleeps—

*Per.* What, is the tyrant jealous?

*Elw.* Hear him, Percy.

*Per.* I will command my rage—Go on.

*Har.* Earl Douglas
Knew, by my arms and my accoutrements,
That I belong'd to you; he question'd much,
And much he menac'd me, but both alike
In vain; he then arrested and confin'd me.

*Per.* Arrest my knight! The Scot shall answer it.

*Elw.* How came you now releas'd?

*Har.* Your noble father
Obtain'd my freedom, having learn'd from Hubert
The news of Percy's death. The good old lord,
Hearing the king's return, has left the castle
To do him homage.
[To Percy] Sir, you had best retire;
Your safety is endanger'd by your stay.
I fear, should Douglas know——

Per. Should Douglas know!
Why what new magic's in the name of Douglas,
That it should strike Northumberland with fear?
Go, seek the haughty Scot, and tell him—no—
Conduct me to his presence.

Elw. Percy, hold;
Think not 'tis Douglas—'tis—

Per. I know it well——
Thou mean'st to tell me 'tis Elwina's husband;
But that inflames me to superior madness.
This happy husband, this triumphant Douglas,
Shall not insult my misery with his bliss.
I'll blast the golden promise of his joys.
Conduct me to him—nay, I will have way—
Come, let us seek this husband.

Elw. Percy, hear me.
When I was robb'd of all my peace of mind,
My cruel fortune left me still one blessing,
One solitary blessing, to console me;
It was my fame.—'Tis a rich jewel, Percy,
And I must keep it spotless, and unsoil'd:
But thou wouldst plunder what e'en Douglas spar'd,
And rob this single gem of all its brightness.

Per. Go—thou wast born to rule the fate of Percy.
Thou art my conqueror still.

Elw. What noise is that?
[Harcourt goes to the side of the stage.

Per. Why art thou thus alarm'd?

Elw. Alas! I feel
The cowardice and terrors of the wicked,
Without their sense of guilt.

Har. My lord, 'tis Douglas.

Elw. Fly, Percy, and for ever!

Per. Fly from Douglas?

Elw. Then stay, barbarian, and at once destroy
My life and fame.

Per. That thought is death. I go:

My honour to thy dearer honour yields.

Elw. Yet, yet thou art not gone!

Per. Farewell, farewell![exit Percy.

Elw. I dare not meet the searching eye of Douglas.
I must conceal my terrors.

Douglas at the side with his sword drawn,
Edric holds him.

Dou. Give me way.

Edr. Thou shalt not enter.

Dou. [struggling with Edric] If there were no hell,
It would defraud my vengeance of its edge,
And she should live.
[breaks from Edric and comes forward.
Cursed chance! he is not here.

Elw. [going.] I dare not meet his fury.

Dou. See she flies
With every mark of guilt.—Go, search the bower,
[aside to Edric.
He shall not thus escape. Madam, return.[aloud.
Now, honest Douglas, learn of her to feign.[aside.
Alone, Elwina? who just parted hence?
[with affected composure.

Elw. My lord, 'twas Harcourt; sure you must have met him.

Dou. O exquisite dissembler! [aside.] No one else!

Elw. My lord!

Dou. How I enjoy her criminal confusion![aside.
You tremble, madam.

Elw. Wherefore should I tremble?
By your permission Harcourt was admitted;
'Twas no mysterious, secret introduction.

Dou. And yet you seem alarm'd.—If Harcourt's presence
Thus agitates each nerve, makes every pulse
Thus wildly throb, and the warm tides of blood
Mount in quick rushing tumults to your cheek;

28

If friendship can excite such strong emotions,
What tremors had a lover's presence caus'd?

Elw. Ungenerous man!

Dou. I feast upon her terrors.[aside.
The story of his death was well contriv'd;[to her.
But it affects not me; I have a wife,
Compar'd with whom cold Dian was unchaste.
[takes her hand.
But mark me well—though it concerns not you—
If there's a sin more deeply black than others,
Distinguish'd from the list of common crimes,
A legion in itself, and doubly dear
To the dark prince of hell, it is—hypocrisy.
[throws her from him, and exit.

Elw. Yes, I will bear his fearful indignation!
Thou melting heart, be firm as adamant;
Ye shatter'd nerves, be strung with manly force,
That I may conquer all my sex's weakness,
Nor let this bleeding bosom lodge one thought,
Cherish one wish, or harbour one desire,
That angels may not hear and Douglas know.[exit.

ACT THE FOURTH.

SCENE I. THE HALL.

Enter Douglas, his sword drawn and bloody in one hand, in the other a letter.
Harcourt, wounded.

Dou. Traitor, no more! this letter shews thy office;
Twice hast thou robb'd me of my dear revenge.
I took thee for thy leader.—Thy base blood
Would stain the noble temper of my sword;
But as the pander to thy master's lust,
Thou justly fall'st by a wrong'd husband's hand.

Har. Thy wife is innocent.

Dou. Take him away.

Har. Percy, revenge my fall![guards bear Harcourt in.

Dou. Now for the letter!

He begs once more to see her.—So 'tis plain
They have already met!—but to the rest——
[Reads.] "In vain you wish me to restore the scarf;
Dear pledge of love, while I have life I'll wear it,
'Tis next my heart; no power shall force it thence;
Whene'er you see it in another's hand,
Conclude me dead."—My curses on them both!
How tamely I peruse my shame! but thus,
Thus let me tear the guilty characters
Which register my infamy; and thus,
Thus would I scatter to the winds of heaven
The vile complotters of my foul dishonour.
[tears the letter in the utmost agitation.

Enter Edric.

Edr. My lord——

Dou. [in the utmost fury, not seeing Edric.] The scarf!

Edr. Lord Douglas.

Dou. [still not hearing him.] Yes, the scarf!
Percy, I thank thee for the glorious thought!
I'll cherish it; 'twill sweeten all my pangs,
And add a higher relish to revenge!

Edr. My lord!

Dou. How! Edric here?

Edr. What new distress?

Dou. Dost thou expect I should recount my shame,
Dwell on each circumstance of my disgrace,
And swell my infamy into a tale?
Rage will not let me—But—my wife is false.

Edr. Art thou convinc'd?

Dou. The chronicles of hell
Cannot produce a falser.—But what news
Of her cursed paramour?

Edr. He has escap'd.

Dou. Hast thou examin'd every avenue?
Each spot? the grove? the bower, her favourite haunt?

30

Edr. I've search'd them all.

Dou. He shall be yet pursued.
Set guards at every gate.—Let none depart
Or gain admittance here, without my knowledge.

Edr. What can their purpose be?

Dou. Is it not clear?
Harcourt has raised his arm against my life;
He fail'd; the blow is now reserv'd for Percy;
Then, with his sword fresh reeking from my heart,
He'll revel with that wanton o'er my tomb;
Nor will he bring her aught she'll hold so dear,
As the curs'd hand with which he slew her husband.
But he shall die! I'll drown my rage in blood,
Which I will offer as a rich libation
On thy infernal altar, black revenge![exeunt.

SCENE II. THE GARDEN.

Enter Elwina.

Elw. Each avenue is so beset with guards,
And lynx-ey'd Jealousy so broad awake,
He cannot pass unseen. Protect him, heaven!

Enter Birtha.

My Birtha, is he safe? has he escap'd?

Bir. I know not. I dispatch'd young Harcourt to him,
To bid him quit the castle, as you order'd,
Restore the scarf, and never see you more.
But how the hard injunction was receiv'd,
Or what has happen'd since, I'm yet to learn.

Elw. O when shall I be eas'd of all my cares,
And in the quiet bosom of the grave
Lay down this weary head!—I'm sick at heart!
Should Douglas intercept his flight!

Bir. Be calm;
Douglas this very moment left the castle,
With seeming peace.

31

Elw. Ah, then, indeed there's danger!
Birtha, whene'er Suspicion feigns to sleep,
'Tis but to make its careless prey secure.

Bir. Should Percy once again entreat to see thee,
'Twere best admit him; from thy lips alone
He will submit to hear his final doom
Of everlasting exile.

Elw. Birtha, no;
If honour would allow the wife of Douglas
To meet his rival, yet I durst not do it.
Percy! too much this rebel heart is thine:
Too deeply should I feel each pang I gave;
I cannot hate—but I will banish—thee.
Inexorable duly, O forgive,
If I can do no more!

Bir. If he remains,
As I suspect, within the castle walls,
'Twere best I sought him out.

Elw. Then tell him, Birtha,
But, Oh! with gentleness, with mercy, tell him,
That we must never, never, meet again.
The purport of my tale must be severe,
But let thy tenderness embalm the wound
My virtue gives. O soften his despair;
But say—we meet no more.

Enter Percy.

Rash man, he's here!
[she attempts to go, he seizes her hand.

Per. I will be heard; nay, fly not; I will speak;
Lost as I am, I will not be denied
The mournful consolation to complain.

Elw. Percy, I charge thee, leave me.

Per. Tyrant, no:
I blush at my obedience, blush to think
I left thee here alone, to brave the danger
I now return to share.

Elw. That danger's past:
Douglas was soon appeas'd; he nothing knows.
Then leave me, I conjure thee, nor again

32

Endanger my repose. Yet, ere thou goest,
Restore the scarf.

Per. Unkind Elwina, never!
'Tis all that's left me of my buried joys,
All which reminds me that I once was happy.
My letter told thee I would ne'er restore it.

Elw. Letter! what letter?

Per. That I sent by Harcourt.

Elw. Which I have ne'er receiv'd. Douglas perhaps—
Who knows?

Bir. Harcourt, t' elude his watchfulness,
Might prudently retire.

Elw. Grant heaven it prove so!
[Elwina going, Percy holds her.

Per. Hear me, Elwina; the most savage honour
Forbids not that poor grace.

Elw. It bids me fly thee.

Per. Then, ere thou goest, if we indeed must part,
To sooth the horrors of eternal exile,
Say but—thou pity'st me!

Elw. [weeps.] O Percy—pity thee!
Imperious honour;—surely I may pity him.
Yet, wherefore pity? no, I envy thee:
For thou hast still the liberty to weep,
In thee 'twill be no crime: thy tears are guiltless,
For they infringe no duty, stain no honour,
And blot no vow; but mine are criminal,
Are drops of shame which wash the cheek of guilt,
And every tear I shed dishonours Douglas.

Per. I swear my jealous love e'en grudges thee
Thy sad pre-eminence in wretchedness.

Elw. Rouse, rouse, my slumb'ring virtue! Percy, hear me.
Heaven, when it gives such high-wrought souls as thine,
Still gives as great occasions to exert them.
If thou wast form'd so noble, great, and gen'rous,
'Twas to surmount the passions which enslave
The gross of human-kind.—Then think, O think,

33

She, whom thou once didst love, is now another's.

Per. Go on—and tell me that that other's Douglas.

Elw. Whate'er his name, he claims respect from me:
His honour's in my keeping, and I hold
The trust so pure, its sanctity is hurt
E'en by thy presence.

Per. Thou again hast conquer'd.
Celestial virtue, like the angel spirit,
Whose flaming sword defended Paradise,
Stands guard on every charm,—Elwina, yes,
To triumph over Douglas, we'll be virtuous.

Elw. 'Tis not enough to be,—we must appear so:
Great souls disdain the shadow of offence,
Nor must their whiteness wear the stain of guilt.

Per. I shall retract—I dare not gaze upon thee;
My feeble virtue staggers, and again
The fiends of jealousy torment and haunt me.
They tear my heart-strings.——Oh!

Elw. No more;
But spare my injur'd honour the affront
To vindicate itself.

Per. But, love!

Elw. But, glory!

Per. Enough! a ray of thy sublimer spirit
Has warm'd my dying honour to a flame!
One effort and 'tis done. The world shall say,
When they shall speak of my disastrous love,
Percy deserv'd Elwina though he lost her.
Fond tears, blind me not yet! a little longer,
Let my sad eyes a little longer gaze,
And leave their last beams here.

Elw. [turns from him.] I do not weep.

Per. Not weep? then why those eyes avoiding mine?
And why that broken voice? those trembling accents?
That sigh which rends my soul?

Elw. No more, no more.

34

Per. That pang decides it. Come—I'll die at once;
Thou Power supreme! take all the length of days,
And all the blessings kept in store for me,
And add to her account.—Yet turn once more,
One little look, one last, short glimpse of day,
And then a long dark night.—Hold, hold, my heart,
O break not yet, while I behold her sweetness;
For after this dear, mournful, tender moment,
I shall have nothing more to do with life.

Elw. I do conjure thee, go.

Per. 'Tis terrible to nature!
With pangs like these the soul and body part!
And thus, but oh, with far less agony,
The poor departing wretch still grasps at being,
Thus clings to life, thus dreads the dark unknown,
Thus struggles to the last to keep his hold;
And when the dire convulsive groan of death
Dislodges the sad spirit—thus it stays,
And fondly hovers o'er the form it lov'd.
Once and no more—farewell, farewell!

Elw. For ever!
[they look at each other for some time,
then exit Percy. After a pause;
'Tis past—the conflict's past! retire, my Birtha,
I would address me to the throne of grace.

Bir. May Heaven restore that peace thy bosom wants!
[exit Birtha.

Elw. [kneels.] Look down, thou, awful, heart-inspecting Judge,
Look down with mercy on thy erring creature,
And teach my soul the lowliness it needs!
And if some sad remains of human weakness
Should sometimes mingle with my best resolves,
O breathe thy spirit on this wayward heart,
And teach me to repent th' intruding sin
In it's first birth of thought!
[Noise within.] What noise is that?
The clash of swords! should Douglas be return'd!

Enter Douglas and Percy, fighting.

Dou. Yield, villain, yield!

Per. Not till this good right arm
Shall fail its master.

Dou. This to thy heart, then.

Per. Defend thy own.
[they fight; Percy disarms Douglas.

Dou. Confusion, death, and hell!

Edr. [without] This way I heard the noise.

Enter Edric, and many Knights and Guards,
from every part of the stage.

Per. Cursed treachery!
But dearly will I sell my life.

Dou. Seize on him.

Per. I'm taken in the toils.
[Percy is surrounded by Guards, who take his sword.

Dou. In the cursed snare
Thou laid'st for me, traitor, thyself art caught.

Elw. He never sought thy life.

Dou. Adulteress, peace!
The villain Harcourt too—but he's at rest.

Per. Douglas, I'm in thy power; but do not triumph,
Percy's betray'd, not conquer'd. Come, dispatch me.

Elw. [to Douglas] O do not, do not, kill him!

Per. Madam, forbear;
For by the glorious shades of my great fathers,
Their godlike spirit is not so extinct,
That I should owe my life to that vile Scot.
Though dangers close me round on every side,
And death besets me, I am Percy still.

Dou. Sorceress, I'll disappoint thee—he shall die,
Thy minion shall expire before thy face,
That I may feast my hatred with your pangs,
And make his dying groans, and thy fond tears,
A banquet for my vengeance.

Elw. Savage tyrant!
I would have fallen a silent sacrifice,

36

So thou had'st spar'd my fame.—I never wrong'd thee.

Per. She knew not of my coming;—I alone
Have been to blame—Spite of her interdiction,
I hither came. She's pure as spotless saints.

Elw. I will not be excus'd by Percy's crime;
So white my innocence, it does not ask
The shade of others' faults to set it off;
Nor shall he need to sully his fair fame
To throw a brighter lustre round my virtue.

Dou. Yet he can only die—but death for honour!
Ye powers of hell, who take malignant joy
In human bloodshed, give me some dire means,
Wild as my hate, and desperate as my wrongs!

Per. Enough of words. Thou know'st I hate thee, Douglas;
'Tis stedfast, fix'd, hereditary hate,
As thine for me; our fathers did bequeath it
As part of our unalienable birthright,
Which nought but death can end.—Come, end it here.

Elw. [kneels] Hold, Douglas, hold!—not for myself I kneel,
I do not plead for Percy, but for thee:
Arm not thy hand against thy future peace,
Spare thy brave breast the tortures of remorse,—
Stain not a life of unpolluted honour,
For, oh! as surely as thou strik'st at Percy,
Thou wilt for ever stab the fame of Douglas.

Per. Finish the bloody work.

Dou. Then take thy wish.

Per. Why dost thou start?
[Percy bares his bosom. Douglas advances
to stab him, and discovers the scarf.

Dou. Her scarf upon his breast!
The blasting sight converts me into stone;
Withers my powers like cowardice or age,
Curdles the blood within my shiv'ring veins,
And palsies my bold arm.

Per. [ironically to the Knights] Hear you, his friends!
Bear witness to the glorious, great exploit,
Record it in the annals of his race,
That Douglas, the renown'd—the valiant Douglas,

Fenc'd round with guards, and safe in his own castle,
Surpris'd a knight unarm'd, and bravely slew him.

Dou. [throwing away his dagger]
'Tis true—I am the very stain of knighthood.
How is my glory dimm'd!

Elw. It blazes brighter!
Douglas was only brave—he now is generous!

Per. This action has restor'd thee to thy rank,
And makes thee worthy to contend with Percy.

Dou. Thy joy will be as short as 'tis insulting.[to Elwina.
And thou, imperious boy, restrain thy boasting.
Thou hast sav'd my honour, not remov'd my hate,
For my soul loaths thee for the obligation.
Give him his sword.

Per. Now thou'rt a noble foe,
And in the field of honour I will meet thee,
As knight encount'ring knight.

Elw. Stay, Percy, stay,
Strike at the wretched cause of all, strike here,
Here sheath thy thirsty sword, but spare my husband.

Dou. Turn, madam, and address those vows to me,
To spare the precious life of him you love.
Even now you triumph in the death of Douglas;
Now your loose fancy kindles at the thought,
And, wildly rioting in lawless hope,
Indulges the adultery of the mind.
But I'll defeat that wish.—Guards, bear her in.
Nay, do not struggle.[she is borne in.

Per. Let our deaths suffice,
And reverence virtue in that form inshrin'd.

Dou. Provoke my rage no farther.—I have kindled
The burning torch of never-dying vengeance
At love's expiring lamp.—But mark me, friends,
If Percy's happier genius should prevail,
And I should fall, give him safe conduct hence,
Be all observance paid him.—Go, I follow thee.
[aside to Edric.
Within I've something for thy private ear.

Per. Now shall this mutual fury be appeas'd!

38

These eager hands shall soon be drench'd in slaughter!
Yes—like two famish'd vultures snuffing blood,
And panting to destroy, we'll rush to combat;
Yet I've the deepest, deadliest, cause of hate,
I am but Percy, thou'rt—Elwina's husband. [exeunt.


## ACT THE FIFTH.

### SCENE I. ELWINA'S APARTMENT.

Elw. Thou who in judgment still remember'st mercy,
Look down upon my woes, preserve my husband!
Preserve my husband! Ah, I dare not ask it;
My very prayers may pull down ruin on me!
If Douglas should survive, what then becomes
Of—him—I dare not name? And if he conquers,
I've slain my husband. Agonizing state!
When I can neither hope, nor think, nor pray,
But guilt involves me. Sure to know the worst
Cannot exceed the torture of suspense,
When each event is big with equal horror.[looks out.
What, no one yet? This solitude is dreadful!
My horrors multiply!

Enter Birtha.

Thou messenger of woe!

Bir. Of woe, indeed!

Elw. How, is my husband dead?
Oh, speak!

Bir. Your husband lives.

Elw. Then farewell, Percy!
He was the tenderest, truest!—Bless him, heaven,
With crowns of glory and immortal joys!

Bir. Still are you wrong; the combat is not over.
Stay, flowing tears, and give me leave to speak.

Elw. Thou sayest that Percy and my husband live;
Then why this sorrow?

Bir. What a task is mine!

Elw. Thou talk'st as if I were a child in grief,
And scarce acquainted with calamity.
Speak out, unfold thy tale, whate'er it be,
For I am so familiar with affliction,
It cannot come in any shape will shock me.

Bir. How shall I speak? Thy husband——

Elw. What of Douglas?

Bir. When all was ready for the fatal combat,
He call'd his chosen knights, then drew his sword,
And on it made them swear a solemn oath,
Confirm'd by every rite religion bids,
That they would see perform'd his last request,
Be it whate'er it would. Alas! they swore.

Elw. What did the dreadful preparation mean?

Bir. Then to their hands he gave a poison'd cup,
Compounded of the deadliest herbs and drugs;
Take this, said he, it is a husband's legacy;
Percy may conquer—and—I have a wife!
If Douglas falls, Elwina must not live.

Elw. Spirit of Herod! Why, 'twas greatly thought!
'Twas worthy of the bosom which conceiv'd it!
Yet 'twas too merciful to be his own.
Yes, Douglas, yes, my husband, I'll obey thee,
And bless thy genius which has found the means
To reconcile thy vengeance with my peace,
The deadly means to make obedience pleasant.

Bir. O spare, for pity spare, my bleeding heart:
Inhuman to the last! Unnatural poison!

Elw. My gentle friend, what is there in a name?
The means are little where the end is kind.
If it disturb thee, do not call it poison;
Call it the sweet oblivion of my cares,
My balm of woe, my cordial of affliction,
The drop of mercy to my fainting soul,
My kind dismission from a world of sorrow,
My cap of bliss, my passport to the skies.

Bir. Hark! what alarm is that?

Elw. The combat's over![Birtha goes out.

[Elwina stands in a fixed attitude, her hands clasped.

Now, gracious heaven, sustain me in the trial,
And bow my spirit to thy great decrees!

Re-enter Birtha.

[Elwina looks stedfastly at her without speaking.

*Bir.* Douglas is fallen.

*Elw.* Bring me the poison.

*Bir.* Never.

*Elw.* Where are the knights? I summon you—approach!
Draw near, ye awful ministers of fate,
Dire instruments of posthumous revenge!
Come—I am ready; but your tardy justice
Defrauds the injur'd dead.—Go, haste, my friend,
See that the castle be securely guarded,
Let every gate be barr'd—prevent his entrance.

*Bir.* Whose entrance?

*Elw.* His—the murderer of my husband.

*Bir.* He's single, we have hosts of friends.

*Elw.* No matter;
Who knows what love and madness may attempt?
But here I swear by all that binds the good,
Never to see him more.—Unhappy Douglas!
O if thy troubled spirit still is conscious
Of our past woes, look down, and hear me swear,
That when the legacy thy rage bequeath'd me
Works at my heart, and conquers struggling nature,
Ev'n in that agony I'll still be faithful.
She who could never love, shall yet obey, thee,
Weep thy hard fate, and die to prove her truth.

*Bir.* O unexampled virtue![a noise without.

*Elw.* Heard you nothing?
By all my fears the insulting conqueror comes.
O save me, shield me!

Enter Douglas.

41

Heaven and earth, my husband!

*Dou.* Yes——
To blast thee with the sight of him thou hat'st,
Of him thou hast wrong'd, adultress, 'tis thy husband.

*Elw.* [kneels.] Blest be the fountain of eternal mercy,
This load of guilt is spar'd me! Douglas lives!
Perhaps both live! [to Birtha.] Could I be sure of that,
The poison were superfluous, joy would kill me.

*Dou.* Be honest now, for once, and curse thy stars;
Curse thy detested fate which brings thee back
A hated husband, when thy guilty soul
Revell'd in fond, imaginary joys
With my too happy rival; when thou flew'st,
To gratify impatient, boundless passion,
And join adulterous lust to bloody murder;
Then to reverse the scene! polluted woman!
Mine is the transport now, and thine the pang.

*Elw.* Whence sprung the false report that thou had'st fall'n?

*Dou.* To give thy guilty breast a deeper wound,
To add a deadlier sting to disappointment,
I rais'd it—I contriv'd—I sent it thee.

*Elw.* Thou seest me bold, but bold in conscious virtue.
—That my sad soul may not be stain'd with blood,
That I may spend my few short hours in peace,
And die in holy hope of Heaven's forgiveness,
Relieve the terrors of my lab'ring breast,
Say I am clear of murder—say he lives,
Say but that little word, that Percy lives,
And Alps and oceans shall divide us ever,
As far as universal space can part us.

*Dou.* Canst thou renounce him?

*Elw.* Tell me that he lives,
And thou shall be the ruler of my fate,
For ever hide me in a convent's gloom,
From cheerful day-light, and the haunts of men,
Where sad austerity and ceaseless prayer
Shall share my uncomplaining day between them.

*Dou.* O, hypocrite! now, Vengeance, to thy office.
I had forgot—Percy commends him to thee,

And by my hand—

Elw. How—by thy hand?

Dou. Has sent thee
This precious pledge of love.[he gives her Percy's scarf.

Elw. Then Percy's dead!

Dou. He is.—O great revenge, thou now art mine!
See how convulsive sorrow rends her frame!
This, this is transport!—injur'd honour now
Receives its vast, its ample retribution.
She sheds no tears, her grief's too highly wrought;
'Tis speechless agony.—She must not faint—
She shall not 'scape her portion of the pain.
No! she shall feel the fulness of distress,
And wake to keen perception of her loss.

Bir. Monster! Barbarian! leave her to her sorrows.

Elw. [in a low broken voice.]
Douglas—think not I faint, because thou see'st
The pale and bloodless cheek of wan despair.
Fail me not yet, my spirits; thou cold heart,
Cherish thy freezing current one short moment,
And bear thy mighty load a little longer.

Dou. Percy, I must avow it, bravely fought,—
Died as a hero should;—but, as he fell,
(Hear it, fond wanton!) call'd upon thy name,
And his last guilty breath sigh'd out—Elwina!
Come—give a loose to rage, and feed thy soul
With wild complaints, and womanish upbraidings.

Elw. [in a low solemn voice.] No.
The sorrow's weak that wastes itself in words,
Mine is substantial anguish—deep, not loud;
I do not rave.—Resentment's the return
Of common souls for common injuries.
Light grief is proud of state, and courts compassion;
But there's a dignity in cureless sorrow,
A sullen grandeur which disdains complaint;
Rage is for little wrongs—Despair is dumb.
[exeunt Elwina and Birtha.

Dou. Why this is well! her sense of woe is strong!
The sharp, keen tooth of gnawing grief devours her,
Feeds on her heart, and pays me back my pangs.

43

Since I must perish 'twill be glorious ruin:
I fall not singly, but, like some proud tower,
I'll crush surrounding objects in the wreck,
And make the devastation wide and dreadful.

Enter Raby.

Raby. O whither shall a wretched father turn?
Where fly for comfort? Douglas, art thou here?
I do not ask for comfort at thy hands.
I'd but one little casket where I lodged
My precious hoard of wealth, and, like an idiot,
I gave my treasure to another's keeping,
Who threw away the gem, nor knew its value,
But left the plunder'd owner quite a beggar.

Dou. What art thou come to see thy race dishonour'd?
And thy bright sun of glory set in blood?
I would have spar'd thy virtues, and thy age,
The knowledge of her infamy.

Raby. 'Tis false.
Had she been base, this sword had drank her blood.

Dou. Ha! dost thou vindicate the wanton?

Raby. Wanton?
Thou hast defam'd a noble lady's honour—
My spotless child—in me behold her champion:
The strength of Hercules will nerve this arm,
When lifted in defence of innocence.
The daughter's virtue for the father's shield,
Will make old Raby still invincible.[offers to draw.

Dou. Forbear.

Raby. Thou dost disdain my feeble arm,
And scorn my age.

Dou. There will be blood enough;
Nor need thy wither'd veins, old lord, be drain'd,
To swell the copious stream.

Raby. Thou wilt not kill her?

Dou. Oh, 'tis a day of horror!

Enter Edric and Birtha.

44

Edr. Where is Douglas?
I come to save him from the deadliest crime
Revenge did ever meditate.

Dou. What meanest thou?

Edr. This instant fly, and save thy guiltless wife.

Dou. Save that perfidious—

Edr. That much-injur'd woman.

Bir. Unfortunate indeed, but O most innocent!

Edr. In the last solemn article of death,
That truth-compelling state, when even bad men
Fear to speak falsely, Percy clear'd her fame.

Dou. I heard him—'Twas the guilty fraud of love.
The scarf, the scarf! that proof of mutual passion,
Given but this day to ratify their crimes!

Bir. What means my lord? This day? That fatal scarf
Was given long since, a toy of childish friendship;
Long ere your marriage, ere you knew Elwina.

Raby. 'Tis I am guilty.

Dou. Ha!

Raby. I,—I alone.
Confusion, honour, pride, parental fondness,
Distract my soul,—Percy was not to blame,
He was—the destin'd husband of Elwina!
He loved her—was belov'd—and I approv'd.
The tale is long.—I chang'd my purpose since,
Forbad their marriage—

Dou. And confirm'd my mis'ry!
Twice did they meet to-day—my wife and Percy.

Raby. I know it.

Dou. Ha! thou knew'st of my dishonour?
Thou wast a witness, an approving witness,
At least a tame one!

Raby. Percy came, 'tis true,
A constant, tender, but a guiltless lover!

45

Dou. I shall grow mad indeed; a guiltless lover!
Percy, the guiltless lover of my wife!

Raby. He knew not she was married.

Dou. How? is't possible?

Raby. Douglas, 'tis true; both, both were innocent;
He of her marriage, she of his return.

Bir. But now, when we believ'd thee dead, she vow'd
Never to see thy rival. Instantly,
Not in a state of momentary passion,
But with a martyr's dignity and calmness,
She bade me bring the poison.

Dou. Had'st thou done it,
Despair had been my portion! Fly, good Birtha,
Find out the suffering saint—describe my penitence,
And paint my vast extravagance of fondness,
Tell her I love as never mortal lov'd—
Tell her I know her virtues, and adore them—
Tell her I come, but dare not seek her presence,
Till she pronounce my pardon.

Bir. I obey.[exit Birtha.

Raby. My child is innocent! ye choirs of saints,
Catch the blest sounds—my child is innocent!

Dou. O I will kneel, and sue for her forgiveness,
And thou shalt help me plead the cause of love,
And thou shalt weep—she cannot sure refuse
A kneeling husband and a weeping father.
Thy venerable cheek is wet already.

Raby. Douglas! it is the dew of grateful joy!
My child is innocent! I now would die,
Lest fortune should grow weary of her kindness,
And grudge me this short transport.

Dou. Where, where, is she?
My fond impatience brooks not her delay;
Quick, let me find her, hush her anxious soul,
And sooth her troubled spirit into peace.

Enter Birtha.

46

Bir. O horror, horror, horror!

Dou. Ah! what mean'st thou?

Bir. Elwina—

Dou. Speak—

Bir. Her grief wrought up to frenzy,
She has, in her delirium, swallow'd poison!

Raby. Frenzy and poison!

Dou. Both a husband's gift;
But thus I do her justice.

As Douglas goes to stab himself, enter Elwina distracted,
her hair dishevelled, Percy's scarf in her hand.

Elw. [goes up to Douglas.]
What, blood again? We cannot kill him twice!
Soft, soft—no violence—he's dead already;—
I did it—Yes—I drown'd him with my tears;
But hide the cruel deed! I'll scratch him out
A shallow grave, and lay the green sod on it;
Ay—and I'll bind the wild briar o'er the turf,
And plant a willow there, a weeping willow—
[she sits on the ground.
But look you tell not Douglas, he'll disturb him;
He'll pluck the willow up—and plant a thorn.
He will not let me sit upon his grave,
And sing all day, and weep and pray all night.

Raby. Dost thou not know me?

Elw. Yes—I do remember
You had a harmless lamb.

Raby. I had indeed!

Elw. From all the flock you chose her out a mate,
In sooth a fair one—you did bid her love it—
But while the shepherd slept, the wolf devour'd it.

Raby. My heart will break. This is too much, too much!

Elw. [smiling.] O 'twas a cordial draught—I drank it all.

Raby. What means my child?

47

Dou. The poison! Oh the poison!
Thou dear wrong'd innocence—

Elw. Off—murderer, off!
Do not defile me with those crimson hands.
[shews the scarf.
This is his winding sheet—I'll wrap him in it—
I wrought it for my love—there—now I've drest him.
How brave he looks! my father will forgive him,
He dearly lov'd him once—but that is over.
See where he comes—beware, my gallant Percy,
Ah! come not here, this is the cave of death,
And there's the dark, dark palace of Revenge!
See the pale king sits on his blood-stain'd throne!
He points to me—I come, I come, I come.
[she faints, they run to her,
Douglas takes up his sword and stabs himself.

Dou. Thus, thus I follow thee.

Edr. Hold thy rash hand!

Dou. It is too late. No remedy but this
Could medicine a disease so desperate.

Raby. Ah, she revives!

Dou. [raising himself.] She lives! bear, bear me to her!
We shall be happy yet.
[he struggles to get to her, but sinks down.
It will not be—
O for a last embrace—Alas! I faint—
She lives——Now death is terrible indeed—
Fair spirit, I lov'd thee—O—Elwina![dies.

Elw. Where have I been? The damps of death are on me.

Raby. Look up, my child! O do not leave me thus!
Pity the anguish of thy aged father.
Hast thou forgot me?

Elw. No—you are my father;
O you are kindly come to close my eyes,
And take the kiss of death from my cold lips!

Raby. Do we meet thus?

Elw. We soon shall meet in peace.ind1

48

I've but a faint remembrance of the past—
But something tells me—O those painful struggles!
Raise me a little—there—[she sees the body of Douglas.
What sight is that?
A sword, and bloody? Ah! and Douglas murder'd!

Edr. Convinc'd too late of your unequall'd virtues,
And wrung with deep compunction for your wrongs,
By his own hand the wretched Douglas fell.

Elw. This adds another, sharper pang to death.
O thou Eternal! take him to thy mercy,
Nor let this sin be on his head, or mine!

Raby. I have undone you all—the crime is mine!
O thou poor injur'd saint, forgive thy father,
He kneels to his wrong'd child.

Elw. Now you are cruel.
Come near, my father, nearer—I would see you,
But mists and darkness cloud my failing sight.
O Death! suspend thy rights for one short moment,
Till I have ta'en a father's last embrace—
A father's blessing.—Once—and now 'tis over.
Receive me to thy mercy, gracious Heaven![she dies.

Raby. She's gone! for ever gone! cold, dead and cold.
Am I a father? Fathers love their children——
I murder mine! With impious pride I snatch'd
The bolt of vengeance from the hand of Heaven.
My punishment is great—but oh! 'tis just.
My soul submissive bows. A righteous God
Has made my crime become my chastisement.[exeunt.
THE END.

Maurice,
Fenchurch Street.

FOOTNOTES

1: Of this estimable lady, a contemporary writer says, "This lady has for many years
flourished in the literary world, which she has richly adorned by a variety of labours, all
possessing strong marks of excellence. In the cause of religion and society, her labours are
original and indefatigable; and the industrious poor have been at once enlightened by her
instructions, and supported by her bounty."

49

As a dramatic writer, Mrs. More is known by her "Search after Happiness," pastoral drama; "The Inflexible Captive,"—"Percy," and "Fatal Falsehood," tragedies; and by her "Sacred Dramas."

Printed in Great Britain
by Amazon

21320297R00031